MAR 4 - 1996

Dream Trains

Dream Trains

Thomas G. Gunning

DILLON PRESS
New York

Maxwell Macmillan Canada
Toronto

Maxwell Macmillan International
New York Oxford Singapore Sydney

To Paige
From Grampy

Photo Credits

Cover photo: SNCF-CAV
Back photos: Rockwell International,
    Norfolk Southern Corporation

Intercity: title page, 24
Thyssenbild: 6, 9, 12
SNCF-CAV: 20, 22, 65
British Railways Board: 26, 27

Norfolk Southern Corporation: 31,
    36, 37
Mi-Jack: 34
Washington Metropolitan Area
    Transit Authority (photo by Larry
    Levine): 40, 42, 43
Rockwell International: 47, 49
G&H SOHO: 55, 59

Dillon Press
Macmillan Publishing Company
866 Third Avenue
New York, NY 10022

Maxwell Macmillan Canada, Inc.
1200 Eglinton Avenue East
Suite 200
Don Mills, Ontario M3C 3N1

Macmillan Publishing Company is part of the Maxwell Communication Group of
Companies

First edition

Printed in the United States of America

10   9   8   7   6   5   4   3   2   1

Library of Congress Cataloging-in-Publication Data

Gunning, Thomas G.
    Dream trains / Thomas G. Gunning. — 1st ed.
        p. cm.
    Includes index.
    Summary: Describes some of the recent advances and future
technological possibilities in railway transportation.
    ISBN 0-87518-558-4
    1. Railroads—Juvenile literature.   [1. Railroads.]   I. Title.
TF148.G85   1992
625.1—dc20   92-9802

Contents

Riding on Air

On a Friday afternoon in 1960, James Powell was stuck in traffic. Stretched before him were miles of cars, trucks, and buses just sitting there.

As he waited, Powell forgot about the cars all around him. He began imagining a land vehicle that would float on waves of electricity. And so the idea for a new kind of train was born. Powerful magnets would create magnetic waves. As if by magic, the magnetic waves would lift the vehicle up off the rails and send it on its way. This new kind of train would be called a Maglev, which is short for "magnetic levitation."

Surprisingly, Powell didn't work with trains or other forms of transportation. He was a

The Transrapid uses very little space and does not carve up the land-scape.

nuclear scientist and had a job with the Brookhaven National Laboratory in New York State.
Nuclear scientists study ways to use the smallest
bits of matter.

Powell discussed his idea with Gordon Danby,
one of his friends at Brookhaven. Danby thought
the idea was a good one. The two spent many
evenings and weekends working on Maglev.
They reported their experiments in scientific
magazines.

Kolm's Magneplane

Other scientists in the United States, England,
Germany, and Japan took note of the work of
Powell and Danby. Scientists from the Japanese
National Railroad flew to the United States to talk
to them. And Henry Kolm, a scientist at the
Massachusetts Institute of Technology, built a toy-
size model of a Maglev vehicle. Kolm called his

The magnets on the underside of the guideway pull the Transrapid up until it rides on a cushion of air.

model a Magneplane. It looked like a jet without wings. Powered by magnets, the small Magneplane zipped around a circular aluminum tube in Kolm's lab. Unfortunately, his lab ran out of money in 1975. Experiments on the Magneplane were halted.

German, English, and Japanese scientists also experimented with magnetically powered vehicles. In 1984 a low-speed Maglev train was built in England. The train didn't go very far. Gliding along on a guideway built above the ground, it only traveled around the airport in the city of Birmingham. But it proved that a Maglev train could work.

Germany and Japan weren't interested in a slow-moving train. They wanted one that would hit speeds of 300 miles (484 kilometers) an hour or more. The two countries also wanted transportation systems that would carry passengers up to 500 miles (805 kilometers). Now the two countries are in a race to see which one will build the better Maglev.

Transrapid

At this point, Germany is outdistancing Japan in Maglev technology. One of Germany's test models, the TR-06, shot down a straight stretch of track at a blazing 256 miles (412 kilometers) an hour. The newest model, the TR-07, is expected to be even faster. Its top speed is 310 miles (500 kilometers) an hour.

Germany's Maglev, which is called Transrapid, doesn't look or even sound like a train. It has no wheels and it glides on a cushion of air above a magnetic guideway rising 23 feet (7 meters) above the ground. Except for a swoosh as it passes by, Transrapid is silent. There is no sound made by wheels rolling on metal and there are no engine noises either; instead, Transrapid has powerful magnets that make it go.

Built into the feet of the Transrapid are support magnets that curve under metal rails on the underside of the guideway. When the current is turned on, the support magnets on the curved feet are pulled up toward the metal rails. The power of the magnetic attraction is strong

The Transrapid is much faster than a conventional train.

enough to pull the Transrapid nearly half an inch (almost a centimeter) up off the guideway but not so strong that its feet actually touch the underside. Guidance magnets on the sides of the feet hold the Transrapid in place so it doesn't sway.

A series of cables are built into the underside of the guideway. When an electric current is sent through them, a magnetic force is created. This is similar to the force a magnet has when it is held close to a piece of metal and pulls the piece of metal to its prongs or poles. The magnetic force in the guideway reacts to the magnets built into the Maglev. The force created by this reaction pulls and pushes the Transrapid along the guideway.

To change the speed of the train, the power

of the current is either increased or decreased. The magnetic pull can be a powerful one. With no wheels to slow it down, a Maglev is much faster than a conventional train with wheels. Despite its speed Transrapid is safe. The train cannot fly off the guideway because of the way its feet wrap around it.

The Transrapid is long lasting and easy to care for. With so few moving parts, there is little to wear out. Because it rides above rather than on the guideway, even that part suffers very little wear and tear. The Transrapid is also very clean. It doesn't burn coal, gas, or oil, so it gives off no smoke or dirt.

Japan's Maglev

The Japanese are also working on a Maglev train. But it works somewhat differently. The Transrapid's magnets work by attracting, or pulling toward, each other. The Japanese Maglev's magnets repel, or push away from, each other. Built into the bottom of the Japanese Maglev are eight coils that are made of special metals known as superconductors. Conductors are materials such as copper and silver that allow electricity to flow through them. Superconductors do a better job than regular ones. Current flows into superconductors more easily than into the electromagnets that Transrapid uses, so the Japanese Maglev produces more magnetic energy. However, magnetic waves produced by a system that repels may be harmful to people, whereas those produced by a system that attracts are safer.

The Japanese Maglev floats along a U-shaped concrete guideway. When the Maglev glides over the coils in the bottom of the guideway, the superconductor magnets create a current that produces a magnetic field. The magnetic field from the guideway repels the one from the

Maglev. This causes the car to rise about 6 inches (15 centimeters). Magnetic waves from the coils in the sides of the guideway push and pull the Maglev along.

The Japanese Maglev isn't nearly ready to be put to use. But the Japanese say that when it is finished, it will be better than the Transrapid. Japan's Maglev trains will probably make more efficient use of magnetic energy and will be faster. One experimental Japanese train has already reached a speed of 323 miles (520 kilometers) an hour. The Japanese believe their Maglev will be the train of the 21st century.

Putting the United States into the Maglev Race

Meanwhile, Kolm, the scientist from Massachusetts Institute of Technology, hasn't given up on his Magneplane idea. He hopes to use it to get the United States back into the Maglev race. Kolm wants to put Magneplane lines above America's highways. A Magneplane system would be cheaper to build than the Maglev lines being planned for Germany and Japan. It would also be less expensive than building new railroad lines or highways. No new land would be needed. Magneplane guideways would be built above the dividing strips of the country's highways.

Instead of using concrete guideways, the Magneplanes would fly slightly more than a foot (less than one-third of a meter) above aluminum guideways. Using superconducting magnets, the Magneplanes would speed passengers on their way at 224 miles (358 kilometers) an hour. Each Magneplane would hold only about 100 passengers, but the entire system would transport a large number of people. Magneplanes would follow one another by just a few miles.

Maglev in the United States

Will Maglevs be accepted in the United States as a safe, efficient way to travel? We'll soon see. A Maglev line is being constructed in central Florida. Able to travel 250 miles (403 kilometers) an hour, this Florida wonder will whisk passengers from the airport in Orlando to International Drive, a main road in Orlando. The trip won't be a long one—just 14 miles (22.5 kilometers)—but it should be enough to see what Maglev travel is really like.

High-Speed Trains

During most of the 1800s and the early 1900s, trains were the main way of traveling long distances on land. But over the years many travelers switched to cars, which were more convenient, or planes, which were much faster. By the 1960s, passenger trains, especially in the United States, seemed to be dying out.

Bullet Trains

The Japanese brought passenger trains back to life with an amazing new train. Each day thousands of people travel 320 miles (512 kilometers) between the cities of Tokyo and Osaka. The old railroad was too slow to make the journey quickly. Besides, many freight trains used the old tracks. The Japanese decided to build brand new ones. They would be specially built for trains traveling at speeds of 130 miles (210 kilometers) an hour. The new train line, which was named Shinkansen (New Fast Railway), made the 320-mile (512-kilometer) trip in just over three hours. The new train had cut the time of the trip in half. With its high speed and pointed nose, the Shinkansen was nicknamed the "Bullet Train."

Bullet Trains were an immediate success. Not only were they swift, but they also ran often and on time. Within just four years, an average of a quarter million passengers were crowding onto the 80 trains that sped between Tokyo and Osaka each day. As the years passed, other trains and lines were added. Today there are 250 trains and four lines carrying 200 million passengers a year.

TGV

The Bullet Train, however, is no longer the fastest passenger train in the world. France now has a train that is even quicker. The 264-mile (426- kilometer) rail line between Paris and Lyons was too slow. More and more people were using planes to make the trip. The French built a straight track and put a sleek, modern electric train on it. The French called this train Train à Grande Vitesse, (TGV), which means "very fast train."

The TGV went into service in the early 1980s. It rocketed along the tracks at an incredible 162 miles (261 kilometers) an hour. It seemed more like a plane than a train. In 1989, an even faster TGV was built which sped between the cities of Paris and Le Mans at 186 miles (300 kilometers) an hour.

The 490-ton electric train was powered by eight 1,500-horsepower motors. The newest TGV had 40 percent more power than the first.

With its powerful motors and sleek wind-cutting design, the TGV could have reached speeds of 223 miles an hour (360 kilometers), but the people in charge were afraid their passengers would be too frightened.

The TGV's sleek, wind-cutting design makes this train one of the fastest in Europe.

In fact, the TGV has proved to be very safe, and it gives a smooth ride. The cars do not rock back and forth. Unless the passengers looked out the window to see the countryside whizzing by, they would have no idea they were traveling so fast.

The Community of European Railways has plans for linking most of the countries of Europe with TGVs or other high-speed trains. By 2015, there will be four times as many train travelers in

The TGV can reach speeds of 223 miles per hour.

that part of the world. Nearly 5,000 miles (8,050 kilometers) of new tracks will have to be constructed. Another 12,000 miles (19,320 kilometers) of track will have to be improved or rebuilt.

APT

There is one big problem with high-speed trains. They can't travel on old tracks. Many of these tracks have too many curves, which makes high-speed travel difficult. A train could take curves at fairly high speed without flying off the tracks, but it might throw riders out of their seats. Great Britain wanted to start a train service similar to the TGV, but British Rail could not afford new tracks, so they created APT (Advanced Passenger Train) in 1981. APT trains are fast but use old tracks. Devices in the APT sense when the train is rounding a curve. Body-shifting equipment then tilts each car inward so the passengers don't

The InterCity is modern, efficient and comfortable.

even realize the train is taking a curve at high speed. With body-tilting devices, APTs travel smoothly at 125 miles (202 kilometers) an hour or more.

In 1989, the APT was replaced by the more powerful InterCity 225. In a test run, the InterCity hit speeds of 162 miles (261 kilometers) an hour. The InterCity also pulled cars that were more modern and comfortable. One of the cars was especially designed so that even passengers in wheelchairs would be able to use it.

The English Channel Tunnel

Despite the success of the InterCity, there is still a major problem with Great Britain's trains: They can't reach France, Spain, Italy, or any of the other countries on the continent of Europe. Great Britain is an island nation. It is separated from France, its nearest neighbor, by a body of water known as the English Channel. However, an old dream is currently underway to join the two countries.

For more than 200 years, engineers have talked of building an undersea tunnel that would link Great Britain and France. A plan created in the 1850s proposed a tunnel-enclosed roadway for horse-drawn carriages. The tunnel was to be lighted with hundreds of candles.

After 27 failed attempts to build it, a successful start was made in 1987. The channel tunnel, minus the candles and carriages, should open for business in 1993.

The tunnel, which is the longest undersea one in the world, covers a distance of more than 32 miles (52 kilometers) and runs from Folkstone, England, to Calais, France. It has three tubes, one for trains from France, another for trains from England, and a service tunnel to repair the other two tunnels in between.

Shuttle trains will carry travelers from one end to the other in 30 minutes or less. On the French side, a TGV will rush passengers to Paris or other cities and towns on the continent. On

A model of the Channel Tunnel station

Shuttle trains will carry passengers through the tunnel in just three hours.

the British side, a regular train will provide a link to London and other cities.

When the system is completed, travelers will be sped from London to Paris in just three hours. If you count the time to and from the airports, that's faster than making the same trip by plane!

In addition to passengers, the tunnel trains will carry cars, buses, and trucks. Cars will be carried in double-deck railroad wagons while buses and trucks will use single-deck railroad cars. Drivers and passengers will stay in their vehicles as they are hauled through the tunnel beneath the water.

High-Speed Travel in the United States

The fastest train in the United States is the Amtrak Metroliner, which speeds along at 125 miles (202 kilometers) an hour between Washington, D.C., and New York City. However, Texas may one day have the fastest train in North America. Investors in Texas are thinking of building a TGV train line between Dallas and Houston. The 245-mile (395-kilometer) trip would take 90 minutes and would be much cheaper than going by plane.

By the year 2000, the number of airline passengers is expected to double. Roads to and from airports will be jammed with cars. With so many planes flying, takeoffs and landings will be delayed. High-speed rail lines could help solve the problem. More travelers would go by train instead of by car or plane. Highways and airports would be less crowded. For trips of 500 miles (805 kilometers) or less, high-speed trains would be the way to travel.

Better Ways
to Haul Freight

The world's trains carry millions of tons of freight each year. In the past, shipping goods by freight train was much slower than shipping by truck. Surprisingly, Malcolm McLean, the owner of a truck company named McLean Transportation, had an idea that helped the railroads speed up their freight deliveries and save money while doing it.

Most of Malcolm McLean's trucks went to the docks, where the boxes or barrels they carried were unloaded and hoisted onto ships. Unloading a truckful of boxes and barrels and

loading them onto a ship took a long time. In
1956 McLean had an idea for a faster way. Why
not pack goods in large containers? At first, he
simply used the trailers from trucks. Later, special containers were built that were hauled by
trucks. A crane lifted the containers and placed
them on the ship, which then carried them to a
distant port. There they were hoisted from the
ship and hitched up to a truck–tractor or placed
on a trailer.

McLean's idea soon spread to the railroads.
By the late 1950s, trains were carrying containers
built for ships. Containers were loaded onto flatcars, or gondolas, and carried by rail to the
docks. Later, the railroads began using railroad
cars built especially to hold containers.

Double Stacks

Railroaders also figured that they could carry
nearly twice as much if they stacked one con-

A double-stack train rounds a corner.

tainer on top of another. These cars are called double stacks. A mile-long double-stack train can carry 200 40-foot (12-meter) containers. A regular mile-long train can haul only 110 containers of the same size.

Double-stack cars are lighter and their sleek sides cut through the wind more easily than regular cars do. Locomotives have an easier time pulling double-stack cars and so use about 40 percent less fuel.

Articulated Cars

In the 1980s, railroaders also started making articulated cars. An articulated car is really five cars built together. They cannot be separated the way regular railroad cars are separated. Except for a coupler at the beginning and end of the unit, the five cars do not have the heavy connectors that regular railroad cars have. This means articulated cars are lighter than regular ones. Because there are fewer couplers, there is less movement and less banging of articulated cars and, therefore, less chance of damage to the freight being carried.

Land Bridges

In the past, when a ship was carrying goods from Japan, which is in the Pacific Ocean, to England, which is in the Atlantic Ocean, it had to pass through the Panama Canal, which connects the

Pacific and Atlantic oceans. The trip through the canal is slow and costly.

Today, many ships from Japan unload their goods at Los Angeles, San Diego, or other West Coast ports that are on the Pacific Ocean. The containers are then carried by train across the United States to New York, Baltimore, or some other East Coast city that is close to the Atlantic Ocean. At that point, the goods are loaded onto a ship that is headed across the Atlantic to England. Surprisingly, shipping the goods across the United States by train is cheaper than sending them by ship through the Panama Canal. In fact, railroads are fast becoming land bridges!

Piggybacking

By acting as land bridges, trains are working more closely with ships. Through piggybacking, the railroads are also cooperating with the trucking industry. Trains can haul some types of goods

Powerful cranes lift the trailers onto flatcars.

more cheaply, especially when the goods are
being sent long distances. But trucks are more
convenient. They can pick up and deliver right to
the farm or warehouse loading dock. Piggybacking uses the advantages of both trains and
trucks. Here's an example of how it works.
Trucks pick up crates of auto parts in Fort Wayne,

Indiana, and drive down to the freight yard, where the truck's trailers are unhitched. Giant cranes lift the trailers onto flatcars. The trailers are carried by train 1,400 miles (2,258 kilometers) to Salt Lake City, Utah. Once there, they are unloaded, hitched to waiting trucks, and driven to warehouses. That's a lot cheaper than having the trailers hauled by trucks all that distance.

RoadRailing

RoadRailing was started to solve problems with piggybacking. Not counting its load, a truck's trailer may weigh 5,000 pounds or more. Flatcars, or container cars, also weigh a great deal. On a piggybacking train, the locomotive is hauling the extra weight of the truck's trailer. But a RoadRailer is both a truck trailer and a railroad freight car. It has a set of train wheels and a set of highway wheels. It also has railroad couplers and a device so that it can be hitched to a truck.

The RoadRailer is a truck trailer and railroad car in one.

A RoadRailer can be used to drive to a farm to pick up a load of fresh vegetables and then drive to the freight yard. The RoadRailer stops on a set of rails. The train wheels are lowered, and the highway wheels are pulled up. The Road-Railer has become a railroad car.

Because a RoadRailer doesn't have to be placed on a container car, the locomotive has less weight to haul, which saves on fuel costs. Today there are over 2,000 RoadRailers in use in the United States and Canada. As fuel costs increase, the railroads are likely to use more and more RoadRailers to carry goods throughout North America.

Once the highway wheels are pulled up and the train wheels lowered, the RoadRailer is ready to ride the tracks.

Trains Are Catching Up

Trucks now transport most of the goods in the
United States. But in the future, the railroads may
carry a larger share of the nation's freight.
Because the country's highways are becoming
more crowded and slower moving, highway trips
will take more than twice as long 20 years from
now, according to the Federal Highway Admin-
istration. Trains, on the other hand, will be
reducing the time of their trips. With better
tracks, lighter cars, faster locomotives, and the
use of computers, freight trains may cut the time
of their trips in half.

City Trains

A growing number of cities in the United States and around the world are building underground railroads to bring people from the suburbs to the city or from one part of the city to another. Fifty years ago there were only 20 underground railroads in the world. Today there are more than 50.

Smart Trains

Whether city railroads run above or underground, they are becoming "smarter." In fact, they're becoming so smart that they soon will be able to run themselves. There will be no need

Underground railroads are an important part of life in both cities and suburbs.

for an engineer to guide the trains or watch their speed. All this will be done by computer. Boxes, located between the tracks, will pick up signals sent out by an approaching train. The signals will tell which train it is, where it's heading, and how fast it's going. These signals will then be sent to a central computer, which will check its memory to see if the train is moving at the right speed. If the train is going too fast, the computer will send a signal through the box that will slow the train down.

The central computer will also keep track of trains arriving in the station. If a train arrives late, the computer will speed it up so it will arrive at the next station on time.

Smart Stations

Train stations will also be smart. They won't need people to sell or even collect tickets. That, too, will be done by computer. To buy a ticket, a passenger will punch a series of buttons to tell the computer where she is going. The price of the ticket will flash on a small screen and the passenger will insert money into a slot. It won't have to be the exact price of the ticket, because a scanning device will "read" the money. It will be able to tell whether the money is real or fake and whether a one-, five-, or ten-dollar bill has been inserted. After "reading" the money, the computer system prints out a ticket and sends the correct change down a metal chute to the passenger.

The passenger will then insert the ticket into a computerized turnstile. A scanner inside the turnstile will read the ticket. If it is okay, a signal will be sent that allows the turnstile to be

People use automated ticket machines in the Washington, D.C. subway system.

Computerized turnstiles are also a common sight in our nation's capital.

turned enough so that one person may pass through. The location of the station will be stamped on the ticket, which will then be returned. When the person arrives at her destination, she will once again insert her ticket into a computerized turnstile. The computer will read the ticket and figure out how much the fare should be. If the ticket is for the exact amount, the turnstile will keep it. If there is money left over, the amount due the traveler will be stamped on the ticket, which again will be returned. All of that will be done in less than three seconds.

Although smart trains and stations may sound

like dreams of the future, they aren't. The Metro that carries passengers in Washington, D.C., is almost completely run by computers and is very similar to the system just described. The main difference is that Washington's Metro has operators on board its trains. Other cities throughout the United States and the world are already following Washington's lead.

People Movers

There's one problem with city trains and underground railways. Once the traveler reaches the city, he has to walk to his destination, catch a cab, or take a bus. Because of this, many commuters prefer driving into the city in their own cars, even if that adds to the city's pollution and traffic. The City of Miami in Florida found a way to solve this problem. A few years ago, Miami started using Metromover. The Metromover is an electrically powered vehicle that runs on a 1.9

mile (3 kilometers) long guideway that stands above the city's roads so that traffic never slows it down.

This driverless people mover loops the center of the city and stops at nine stations. Running just a few minutes apart, the Metromovers are more convenient than buses and cheaper than cabs.

Metromover is especially handy for Metrorail riders. The Metrorail is a fast-moving commuter train that rushes passengers into Miami from surrounding towns and suburbs. Metromover is just a short walk from the platform where Metrorail stops. Metrorail passengers ride the Metromover for free. Others pay just 25 cents. Some 12,000 passengers ride this people mover each day.

People movers can also be found at some airports. One is now being planned to run among the terminals at Chicago's O'Hare International Airport. Using an automated guideway, the people mover will run 24 hours a day and is expected to carry up to 2,400 people an hour.

Computerized Trains

The biggest change in trains is one that most people don't even notice. That change is computers. They have been used by the railroads for a number of years to keep track of trains and to make up train schedules. But in the years to come, computers will be used to help with just about every job in railroading. They will even be used to operate locomotives.

Computerized Classification Yards

One of the toughest jobs in railroading is getting a train's cars together. Imagine this: There is a giant yard with dozens of sets of tracks. Each day,

some 1,500 cars are pulled into the yard. The
cars have to be sorted out so that each one is
attached to the right train. They must be
unhooked from the trains that brought them and
then coupled to trains that will take them where
they are supposed to go. All this must be done

A classification yard at night

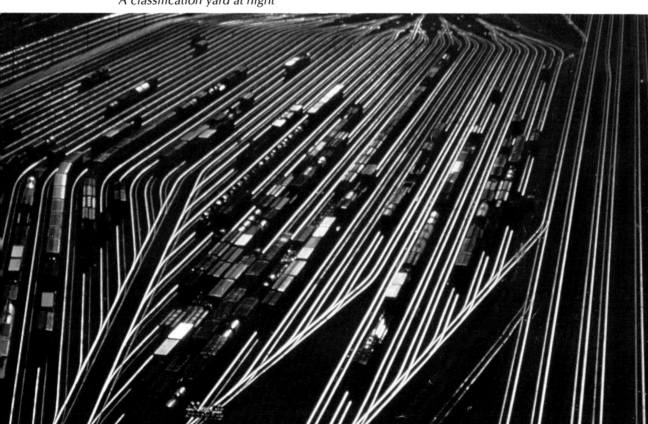

quickly and with no mistakes. A farmer shipping
lettuce meant for Massachusetts doesn't want it
sent to Virginia by mistake. The lettuce could
lose its freshness if it were sent to the wrong
place before being transported onward to Massachusetts.

The area where railroad cars are sorted is
known as a classification yard. Up until about
the 1940s, switch engines moved cars from one
train to another in most classification yards.
That took lots of time and money. Later, special
hump yard tracks were constructed. A hump, or
small hill, was built into the yard. Below were
six, seven, or maybe even a dozen sets of tracks.
A switch engine would push a line of cars up
over the hump. Each car would be uncoupled as
it passed over the hill. Switches were set by a
tower operator so the car would roll down onto
the set of tracks where other cars that would
make up the same train were waiting. Brake
shoes built into the tracks pressed against the

Advanced computers give the railroad dispatcher tremendous control over every train and track in his territory.

wheels of the cars to slow them down so the cars wouldn't jump the tracks or go crashing into one another.

Computers are now being used in many yards to direct railroad cars to the correct set of tracks. The computer also controls the brake shoes in the tracks. It gets information from a scale that weighs the car, and from radar that measures wind speed. Taking weight and wind speed into account, the computer adjusts the car's brake shoes so that it rolls between 2 and 3 miles (3.2 and 4.8 kilometers) an hour. Other devices check for bent wheels, broken parts, or other kinds of damage. Damaged cars are directed to the repair yard.

The computer speeds cars on their way so that trains can be assembled sooner and so deliver their goods quicker. Because fewer workers are needed to direct freight cars, the railroads save money. They are then able to offer cheaper and faster service.

Transponders

In the future, computers will also keep track of the railroad's freight cars and locomotives. Special devices known as transponder tags would be placed on locomotives and freight cars. Radio readers set up alongside or between the tracks would send out radio waves. Picking up the waves from the reader as the locomotive and freight cars roll by, transponder tags would send back signals that would identify the locomotive and cars to which they were attached. The reader would then send the information back to a central computer. In this way, the central computer would "know" the location of the railroad's locomotives and freight cars even if they were on the move.

The toughest part of putting the transponder system into operation would be putting transponder tags on the 1,300,000 freight cars and 21,000 locomotives in the United States. These cars are owned by dozens of railroad companies, which would have to agree that the benefits outweigh the costs of outfitting all those trains.

Computer Control System

In addition to using transponders, modern trains will have a computer control system that will let railroad dispatchers know precisely where a train is and how fast it is going. Working with computers placed on board each locomotive, the system could actually control the train. If it were late, signals from the computer could speed it up. If it were overtaking another train, other signals could slow it down. Or the train up ahead could be shuttled onto a side track until it was passed by the faster train.

The computer control system would also make emergency stops. If there were a fallen tree on the tracks, the computer would pick up a signal and stop the train.

The computer system would also check the train itself. Onboard monitors would give the fuel level, temperature, and speed of the locomotive as well as displaying a warning if something were wrong with the locomotive and indicating what the problem was. A light would flash if the engine were overheating or if a part were wearing out. On some systems a computer voice would call attention to the problem. Trains might still have engineers—at least for a while—but mostly they would be just watching over the dials and computer monitors to make sure that everything was okay.

Central Dispatching Headquarters

Each railroad will have a central dispatching headquarters, which are already in use in some areas. A giant rounded screen that curves around a large circular room will show where all the railroad's trains are. Colored lights will give information about each train's journey. Green, for instance, means that the train is on time. Yellow indicates the train is up to an hour late; red indicates that a train is more than an hour late. From the dispatching headquarters, workers will be able to regulate dozens of trains running on thousands of miles of tracks.

Underground Trains
of the Future

In the future there won't be any room for new highways or railways. That land will be needed for homes, farms, and factories. But there will be more people and goods than ever that need to be moved from place to place. How will they be transported? Underground.

Air Pressure Train

In the years to come, more use will be made of tunnels and underground tubes. Tomorrow's

trains might use a device that was invented
nearly 150 years ago by Isambard Kingdom
Brunel, an English engineer and transportation

A drawing of the "Air Gulper" arriving at its destination

whiz. Brunel designed the first ocean steamer, a tunnel, a suspension bridge, and several railways.

In 1844, while working on railways, Brunel tested out a system that used air pressure to push a train through a large iron tube. The train was bolted onto a large piston. A piston is a round piece of metal that slips back and forth in a tube. Air was pumped out of the tube in front of the train. Because there was no air to hold it back, air pressure behind the piston pushed the piston and the attached train forward.

Brunel's experimental train ran from Exeter to Newton Abbot in Devon, England. However, the train sometimes broke down. The problem was that air leaked out of the tube. In order for the train to be pushed forward, the seal between the piston and the tube had to be air-tight. Brunel had difficulty keeping the seal as tight as it needed to be. The air pressure train had to be shut down. It was one of Brunel's few failures.

Air Gulper

Although Brunel's air pressure train didn't work, it wasn't a bad idea. A number of scientists in the United States and Europe are working on his plan with some changes. One such underground railway idea is known as Project Tubeflight. As a vehicle speeds through a tube, it sucks in the air and heats it. Heated air expands, which means it grows larger and takes up more space. The expanded air is then forced out of the back of the engine. This shoots the tube vehicle forward. Because it takes in so much air, the vehicle has been nicknamed Air Gulper.

A 2,000-foot (617-meter) tunnel has been built at Rensselaer Polytechnic Institute to test this system. It is expected that the Gulper could hit speeds of up to 500 miles (805 kilometers) an hour. The Gulper would be used to travel between large cities that are anywhere from a few hundred to a thousand miles apart.

Planetran

The Air Gulper might sound fast, but the Planetran would make the Gulper look as though it were standing still. The Planetran has been contrived by Robert M. Salter, a scientist at the famous Rand Corporation. Planetran would rocket across the United States at a top speed of 14,000 miles (22,581 kilometers) an hour. Passengers boarding Planetran in New York would reach Los Angeles, nearly 2,500 miles (4,032 kilometers) away, in just 21 minutes. Planetran will pick up speed and slow down gradually so that passengers won't be jolted. With no air pressure outside to push against Planetran, passengers inside pressurized cars will hardly be aware that they are racing across the country at spaceship speed.

Shaped like a long, thin cigar with a tip at each end, Planetran will be powered by super-magnets. Powerful magnetic waves coming from

A diagram of the two-way Planetran System

Planetran guideways will meet powerful magnetic waves coming from Planetran's cars. The force of the waves pushing against one another will lift Planetran up off the guideway and shoot it forward.

Planetran will speed through long tubes built into plastic-coated tunnels up to a mile underground. To keep Planetran from rocking back and forth, the tunnels will need to be arrow straight.

Vacuum pumps built into the tunnel would suck out just about all the air. One of the reasons Planetran would be able to reach such high speeds is that there will be little air to hold it back or slow it down.

Planetran stations would be located in major cities. Where possible, the stations would be next to train, bus, and subway stops and airports. Passengers would be able to hop off mass transit and walk over to a Planetran terminal.

At first, Planetran will cross the United States from east to west, most likely from New York to Los Angeles, with a stop at Dallas and, later, one at Chicago. In time, routes would be built north and south.

Being underground, Planetran wouldn't pollute the air or add to the noise in our towns and cities. And it wouldn't take up valuable land that is needed for homes, farms, or factories. In fact, Planetran tunnels could save land. Phone and electric lines and gas pipelines that are now placed aboveground could be built into the tunnels. That way they wouldn't take up useful space.

There is one problem with Planetran—the tunnel. Building such a long tunnel deep underground would be expensive. The cost of building one between New York and Los Angeles would be about $200 billion. And that's not including terminals.

To cut through the hard rock deep underground, laser beams and high-powered jets of water would be used. The hardest of rock would be melted by Subterrene. Subterrene is a drill that produces such intense heat at its tip that it turns the hardest of rock into a red-hot liquid.

When the tunnel is completed, the tubes for Planetran would be assembled. High-speed trains would be used to carry them into the tunnels.

Once Planetran was finished, there would be fewer planes in the air. Many people who once traveled by plane would be rocketing across the country far beneath the ground.

Will Planetran ever be built? At this point, it might sound like a strange idea. But then not so many years ago, landing men on the moon sounded like an impossible dream.

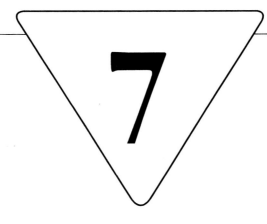

Trains in Tomorrow's World

Tomorrow's trains will be sleeker, faster, and safer. With guidance by computers, they will also just about run themselves. High-speed trains will rocket down the rails at speeds of 300 miles (484 kilometers) an hour. Large Maglevs will glide along overhead guideways at speeds approaching 500 miles (805 kilometers) an hour. Personal-size Maglevs might be used as people movers. Known as People Pods, they will carry just two passengers and will only hit speeds of 100 miles (161 kilometers) an hour. Passengers will board the People Pods at special stations. After punching in their destination, the passengers will be whisked on their way.

Freight Trains of the Future

Because of crowded highways and air pollution, there will be fewer trucks in the world of the future. Mile-long freight trains made up of double-stack cars will do most of the country's long-distance hauling. Trucks will be used mainly for short runs. Much of the power used to run the trains will be produced by solar cells, which change the sun's rays into electricity.

Underground Travel

In time, land will become very scarce. It will be too valuable to use for railroad tracks or guideways for Maglevs. Before the end of the 21st century, tunnels will be built across the country.

The trains of today were once the dream trains of tomorrow.

Underground Maglev trains will speed from coast to coast in under an hour. If the cross-country tunnels are a success, tunnels may be built under the Atlantic Ocean to connect the United States with Europe and, later, under the Pacific Ocean, to connect the United States with Asia.

In the next century, airlines and buses will lose much of their business to the railroads. The fastest, safest, most comfortable way to travel between cities and across the country will be by train.

A Dream Train Time Line

1804   A locomotive invented by Richard Trevithick hauls wagons loaded with ten tons of iron ore and 70 men.

1825   The world's first public railroad runs between the towns of Stockton and Darlington, England.
The first monorail begins operation.
America's first rail locomotive runs on a half-mile test track in Hoboken, New Jersey.

1829   An English locomotive known as the Stourbridge Lion becomes the first steam engine to run on commercial tracks.

1830   The Liverpool and Manchester Railway of England, which carries both passengers and freight, begins operating.
Peter Cooper's locomotive, the Tom Thumb, makes a test run from Baltimore, Maryland, to Ellicott's Mills, Maryland, and back again.

1831   United States mail is carried by the railroad for the first time.

1837   The world's first sleeping car operates between Harrisburg, Pennsylvania, and Chambersburg, Pennsylvania.

1844   Isambard Kingdom Brunel devises an air pressure railway in England.

1851   The telegraph is used to dispatch trains.
1855   Railroads hire the first woman employee, Susan Morningstar.
1859   The first Pullman sleeping car goes into operation.
1863   Dining cars are introduced.
1869   George Westinghouse applies for a patent for air brakes.
1883   Trains begin operating on standard time.
1887   Electric lights are used on passenger trains.
1893   Locomotive 999 becomes the first to hit 100 miles (161 kilometers) an hour.
1925   First diesel-electric locomotive is used to switch cars.
1955   Railroads begin using computers.
1964   Japan's high-speed Bullet Train begins service between Tokyo and Osaka.
1971   Amtrak begins operating most United States intercity passenger trains.
1981   France's TGV goes into service.
       British Rails creates the APT.
1984   A low-speed Maglev train begins operation in England.
1987   Work on the English Channel tunnel is started.
1988   The Transrapid, a high-speed Maglev train, hits 256 miles (412 kilometers) an hour.
       The InterCity replaces the APT.
1993   The tunnel connecting France and England is due to be completed.

Glossary

articulated cable: railroad car made up of movable sections

attract: pull toward

cable: wire made especially to carry electricity

classification yard: area in which cars are separated according to the train they will be hooked up to

coil: electrical device made up of wire twisted into a circular shape

conductor: material, such as copper or silver, that allows electricity to flow through

current: the flow of electricity

double-stacks: railroad cars that have one container placed on top of another

electromagnet: metal that becomes a magnet when electricity is sent into the wire that surrounds it

engineer: person who operates a locomotive

gondola: an open freight car with low sides

iron highway: long platform type of freight car that has a loading ramp

locomotive: engine used to push or pull railroad cars along a track monitor: set with a TV-type screen that shows signals and messages sent by a computer

piggyback: carrying truck trailers on railroad cars

piston: round piece of metal pushed back and forth in a tube

radio reader: device that sends out radio waves, receives returning signals, interprets the signals, and sends them to a central computer

superconductor: material that provides a very easy path for electricity to flow through

switch engine: locomotive used to move railroad cars from one train to another

transponder: device that receives radio waves and then sends out signals

Index

About the Author

Thomas Gunning currently teaches graduate courses in reading methods at Southern Connecticut State University. He has also worked as a reading consultant, editor, and reading and English teacher. Dr. Gunning has served as the president of the Connecticut Association for Reading Research, and is a member of the International Reading Association and the National Council of Teachers of English. Thomas Gunning is the author of many books for young readers, including DREAM CARS and DREAM PLANES for Dillon Press. He and his family reside in Newington, Connecticut.